3rd & Bird

FLY MUFFIN!

Follow the words along the bottom of each page and sing the theme song out loud.

Welcome to 3rd & Bird!
We've got the best branches and
the best birds, it's the place to be!

Everybirdy around here loves to sing.
You can join in the songs, too!

One day, Muffin hopped over to her older brother, Samuel. She had a big idea. She really wanted to...

3rd! 3rd & Bird!

Where the birdies meet,

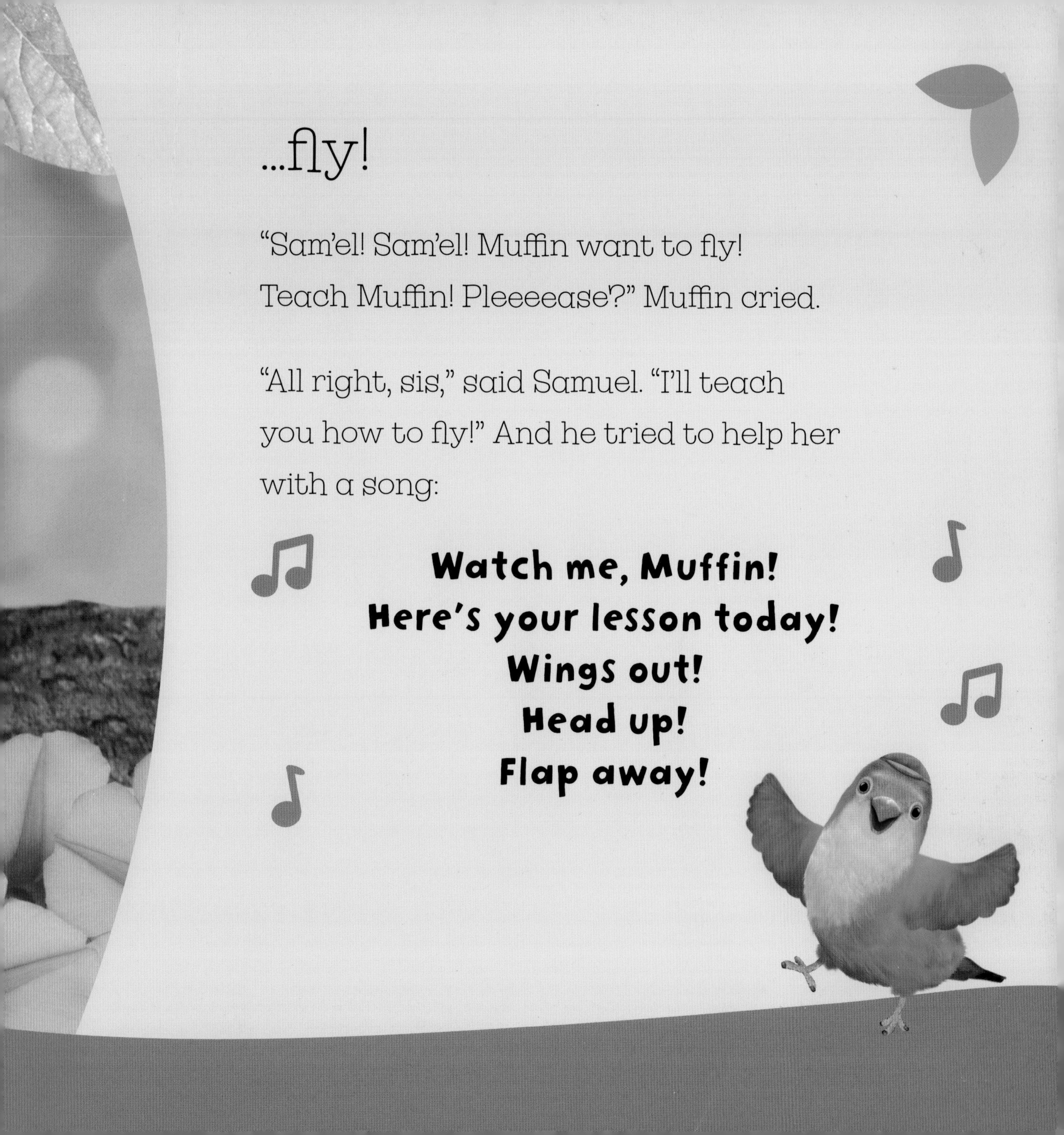

...fly!

"Sam'el! Sam'el! Muffin want to fly! Teach Muffin! Pleeeease?" Muffin cried.

"All right, sis," said Samuel. "I'll teach you how to fly!" And he tried to help her with a song:

Watch me, Muffin!
Here's your lesson today!
Wings out!
Head up!
Flap away!

Muffin put her wings out, her head up and flapped away... but she **still** couldn't fly.

"Muffin fall down, go boom," she said sadly.

"There must be someone on 3rd & Bird who can help us," said Samuel. So together they went to see Samuel's best friend, Rudy.

"Hi, Rudy!" said Samuel. He sang:

My little sister Muffin
Really wants to fly!
Do you think you can help her?

"Sure. I'll give it a try," cried Rudy.

Just above the street,

To sing tweedle-ee-deet!

We'll put her on my kite,
She'll fly into the air,
And soon our little Muffin
Will be flying everywhere!

But Muffin was too **heavy** for Rudy's kite.

"Let's go and see Missy. Maybe she can help Muffin fly," said Samuel, and they set off to visit Missy.

Missy said she had the perfect way for Muffin to fly – on her trapeze!

"Muffin fly!" said Muffin and hopped on the trapeze.

It felt wobbly on Missy's trapeze.

"Muffin fall!" cried Muffin. She was too frightened to let go, so Samuel helped her back down.

3rd! 3rd & Bird,

Where a bird or two,

Just then, the young birds saw Mr Beakman flying by the branch and called him over.

"Beaky!" said Muffin.

"Hello, Samuel, Muffin and Rudy," said Mr Beakman. "What seems to be the problem?"

Muffin sighed loudly.

When Muffin try
To go zoom-zoom...
Muffin no fly!
Muffin just fall
Down and go boom!

Mr Beakman nodded his beak. "I'm afraid your wings are too small, Muffin," he said. "But there are other ways to fly. There's **always** a way!"

Can play peek-a-boo

On the Avenue.

Mr Beakman pointed to a little ant.

Imagine you're an ant
Climbing up a tree,
Carrying a breadcrumb
That's as heavy as can be!
Well, little ant,
Believe me when I say:
Don't give up,
keep on trying...
There's always a way!

And the ant raced along!

Mr Beakman then pointed to a spider trapped in its own web.

Imagine you're a spider
Spinning your own web—
You try to catch a fly,
But you get caught instead!
Well, little spider,
Believe me when I say:
Don't give up,
keep on trying...
There's always a way!

And the spider broke free!

On 3rd!

3rd!

"Remember, there is always
a way. Toodles!" cried
Mr Beakman cheerfully,
and he flew away.

Samuel thought **hard** about
their problem.

"I've got it!" he said at last.
"We can put Missy's trapeze
and Rudy's kite together,
to make...

...a kite-apeze!"

Muffin climbed aboard the kite-apeze, and a gust of wind lifted her into the air. whoosh!

"Muffin fly...!" said Muffin happily, as she flew high in the sky.

Muffin and Samuel's parents looked up from their branch in the tree. They felt very proud of little Muffin.

3rd!

And Samuel, Rudy and Muffin flew
through 3rd & Bird, singing:

Muffin kept trying
Now Muffin is flying
Flying in her kite-apeze!

The end

3rd & Bird

Follow the words along the bottom of each page and sing the theme song out loud.

Welcome to 3rd & Bird!
We've got the best branches and
the best birds, it's the place to be!

Everybirdy around here loves to sing.
You can join in the songs, too!

One day, Muffin hopped over to her older brother, Samuel. She had a big idea. She really wanted to...

3rd! 3rd & Bird!

Where the birdies meet,

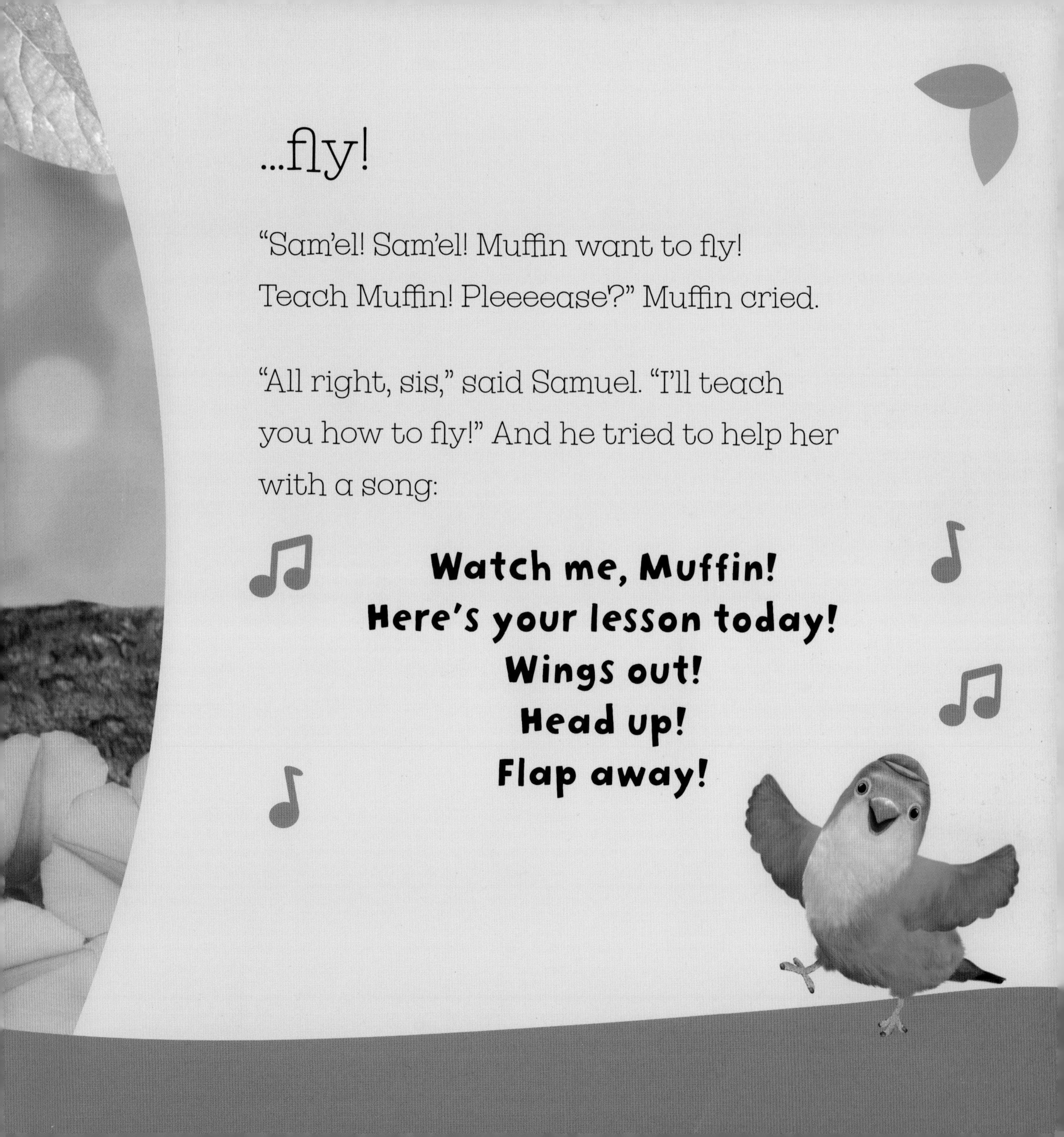

...fly!

"Sam'el! Sam'el! Muffin want to fly! Teach Muffin! Pleeeease?" Muffin cried.

"All right, sis," said Samuel. "I'll teach you how to fly!" And he tried to help her with a song:

Watch me, Muffin!
Here's your lesson today!
Wings out!
Head up!
Flap away!

Muffin put her wings out, her head up and flapped away... but she **still** couldn't fly.

"Muffin fall down, go boom," she said sadly.

"There must be someone on 3rd & Bird who can help us," said Samuel. So together they went to see Samuel's best friend, Rudy.

"Hi, Rudy!" said Samuel. He sang:

My little sister Muffin
Really wants to fly!
Do you think you can help her?

"Sure. I'll give it a try," cried Rudy.

Just above the street,

To sing tweedle-ee-deet!

We'll put her on my kite,
She'll fly into the air,
And soon our little Muffin
Will be flying everywhere!

But Muffin was too **heavy** for Rudy's kite.

"Let's go and see Missy. Maybe she can help Muffin fly," said Samuel, and they set off to visit Missy.

Missy said she had the perfect way for Muffin to fly - on her trapeze!

"Muffin fly!" said Muffin and hopped on the trapeze.

It felt wobbly on Missy's trapeze.

"Muffin fall!" cried Muffin. She was too frightened to let go, so Samuel helped her back down.

3rd! 3rd & Bird,

Where a bird or two,

Just then, the young birds saw Mr Beakman flying by the branch and called him over.

"Beaky!" said Muffin.

"Hello, Samuel, Muffin and Rudy," said Mr Beakman. "What seems to be the problem?"

Muffin sighed loudly.

When Muffin try
To go zoom-zoom...
Muffin no fly!
Muffin just fall
Down and go boom!

Mr Beakman nodded his beak. "I'm afraid your wings are too small, Muffin," he said. "But there are other ways to fly. There's **always** a way!"

Can play peek-a-boo

On the Avenue.

Mr Beakman pointed to a little ant.

Imagine you're an ant
Climbing up a tree,
Carrying a breadcrumb
That's as heavy as can be!
Well, little ant,
Believe me when I say:
Don't give up,
keep on trying...
There's always a way!

And the ant raced along!

Mr Beakman then pointed to a spider trapped in its own web.

Imagine you're a spider
Spinning your own web—
You try to catch a fly,
But you get caught instead!
Well, little spider,
Believe me when I say:
Don't give up,
keep on trying...
There's always a way!

And the spider broke free!

On 3rd!

3rd!

"Remember, there is always a way. Toodles!" cried Mr Beakman cheerfully, and he flew away.

Samuel thought **hard** about their problem.

"I've got it!" he said at last. "We can put Missy's trapeze and Rudy's kite together, to make..."

...a kite-apeze!"

Muffin climbed aboard the kite-apeze, and a gust of wind lifted her into the air. whoosh!

"Muffin fly...!" said Muffin happily, as she flew high in the sky.

Muffin and Samuel's parents looked up from their branch in the tree. They felt very proud of little Muffin.

3rd!

And Samuel, Rudy and Muffin flew through 3rd & Bird, singing:

Muffin kept trying
Now Muffin is flying
Flying in her kite-apeze!

The end